Shakesp

Greatest Stories

Abridged and Illustrated

THE MERCHANT OF VENICE

Wonder House

Wonder House

(An imprint of Prakash Books)

contact@wonderhousebooks.com

ISBN : 9789389432497

Cover image: https://commons. wikimedia.org/wiki/ File:Shakespeare%27s comedy_of_the_Merchant of Venice _(1914)_(14765085805).jpg

ABOUT THE AUTHOR

William Shakespeare

William Shakespeare is undoubtedly one of the greatest playwrights to have ever lived. He gained fame for his excellent ability to portray human emotions in the form of comedies, tragedies, tragic-comedies and historical plays. Some of his greatest plays include *Macbeth, Hamlet, Romeo and Juliet, The Merchant of Venice, A Midsummer Night's Dream, Julius Caesar, As You Like It, Othello, The Tempest*, and many more. He has been credited with giving the world a plethora of new words and phrases, which are used in our daily language today.

Popularly known as the "Bard of Avon", Shakespeare's contributions to literature are numerous and significant. Apart from plays, he also wrote sonnets and poems. Along with being a writer, Shakespeare was also a co-owner of a theatrical company named Lord Chamberlain's Men. Later, he became a co-owner of The Globe Theatre, which was built in 1599. The Globe is still one of the most cherished theatres in the world and manages to put up thrilling productions of Shakespeare's best works even today.

CAST LIST

The Merchant of Venice

Shylock:	A Jewish moneylender
Portia:	A wealthy, intelligent and beautiful heiress
Antonio:	A merchant and Bassanio's best friend
Bassanio:	A kinsman and dear friend of Antonio
Jessica:	Shylock's daughter
Gratiano:	A friend of Bassanio
Nerissa:	Portia's confidante and lady-in-waiting
Lorenzo:	A common friend of Antonio and Bassanio
The Prince of Morocco:	Portia's suitor
Launcelot:	Shylock's servant
The Prince of Arragon:	A Spanish nobleman
Solanio:	A Venetian gentleman
Salarino:	A friend of Antonio
Old Gobbo:	Launcelot's father and a servant
Doctor Bellario:	Portia's cousin and a wealthy Paduan lawyer
Balthasar:	Portia's servant

“

So can I give no reason, nor I will not,
More than a lodged hate and a certain loathing
I bear Antonio, that I follow thus
A losing suit against him. Are you answered?

”

– **Shylock**, Act IV, Scene 1

One fine evening, in the city of Venice, a middle-aged man was standing on a bridge, gazing out at the canal. It was a very successful merchant of Venice called Antonio.

Antonio was famous amongst the Christians for three reasons—first, his wealth which was growing day by day; second, his gracious attitude; and third, his everlasting melancholic behaviour. Antonio firmly believed that life

was a stage where every person had a part to play, and he played the sad one.

His beloved friends, Solanio and Salarino, chanced upon him on the bridge.

Salarino sensed Antonio's mood and asked, "Friend, are you still worried about your ships?"

Before Antonio could reply, Solanio said, "Believe me, Antonio, if I had invested all my money in the cargo business, I would also be tossing blades of grass in the air to see which way the wind is blowing."

After listening to them patiently, Antonio replied, "No, friends, I am not worried about my money. I am generally this sad. It's in my nature."

Salarino refused to believe his words. "I think you're in love, but your lover is not in love with your love!"

Antonio simply rolled his eyes and denied the theory. Meanwhile, Bassanio, Lorenzo and Gratiano were crossing the bridge when Salarino saw them. He said, "Antonio, I guess you have other guests to entertain. We'll take your leave."

Antonio thanked Salarino and Solanio for their concern and bid them farewell. Salarino stopped to greet Bassanio, Lorenzo and Gratiano.

"Friends, let's make a plan to meet soon and enjoy each other's company," said Bassanio.

Salarino and Solanio agreed. "Yes, it's been days since we've had a meal together. Let's plan something then."

After some small talk the two of them left. Lorenzo and Gratiano were about to leave the two best friends, Bassanio and Antonio, alone when Gratiano piped up, "Antonio, you don't look well. Are you okay?"

Antonio was frustrated with this question by now and chose to ignore it. But Gratiano continued pestering him, "Antonio, I have seen men who are always quiet. They are generally very silent and stern. These kind of men behave like they are important and respected in the society.

So, they choose to stay quiet. I'm sure if they were to open their mouths people would realise they are actually fools. Anyway, I will leave now."

"Okay, we'll meet at dinnertime," said Lorenzo. "I must be the so-called wise man that you keep talking about, since you never let me speak."

"If you spend two more years with me, you'll forget the sound of your own voice. Because I talk a lot and everyone should talk, it's important ..." Gratiano was cut off mid-sentence.

"Goodbye, Gratiano. Thanks to your lecture, I'll try and speak more from now on," said Antonio.

As they left, Antonio turned to Bassanio with a look of horror and asked, "Seriously, what was that?"

Bassanio laughed. "Don't worry. Gratiano always talks more than he should. His ideas are like trying to find a needle in a haystack. And when you find it you realise it was not worth the trouble!"

Antonio smiled, waiting to change the subject. "Bassanio, who is the girl you love? You promised to tell me!"

"His ideas are like trying to find a needle in a haystack. And when you find it you realise it was not worth the trouble!"

Bassanio began hesitantly, "Antonio, you know that I am not financially stable and I am already living way beyond my means. I have a lot of debt to clear. And, indeed, I owe you the most—money and gratitude, both. I know that you love me and worry about me. So, I am sure you'll let me explain my plan to pay back my debts." Antonio gently replied, "Yes, of course, Bassanio, carry on. I am all ears!"

"Antonio, when I was a schoolboy, I lost one of my arrows. So, to get that arrow back, I shot another arrow in the same direction and watched it with more concentration—this is how I got my first arrow back. I am telling you this story because I know I owe you a lot. And like a small child, I have once again lost what I owe. So I need your help to find it. If you give me some more money, I will utilise it in the same way. Either I will return both the amounts, or only the amount you pay me right now. And I'll still owe you what I originally did."

Antonio heard him out and gently patted his back. "Bassanio, you know me, I trust you. I know you will return my money soon, but by explaining your plan like this I feel like you're doubting my friendship. Just tell me what you want and when, I will arrange it right away."

Bassanio suddenly turned shy. "Antonio, there is this girl I met in Belmont. She is gorgeous, intelligent and wealthy.

Her name is Portia. Men from around the world visit Belmont only to see her beauty. But, she has never accepted anyone's proposal. I love her, and I know that she feels the same for me. Unfortunately, I don't have enough money to hold my own in front of her suitors."

> "Men from around the world visit Belmont only to see her beauty."

Antonio sighed, "Bassanio you know I would lend you the money if I could. But all of my fortune is tied up in the cargo business, and all the ships are at sea. I'll get my profit when the ships reach the ports. Till then, I can only help you with my words."

He added as an afterthought, "Why don't you borrow money from other merchants? I'll be the guarantor; I'll do whatever I can to get your loan sanctioned. I'll repay the loan amount, and you can pay me back later."

Bassanio gratefully agreed to the plan, overwhelmed by Antonio's love and support.

While Bassanio and Antonio were planning their journey to Belmont to meet Portia, Portia and her maid Nerissa were getting tired of meeting men with low intelligence, high confidence and less than average looks.

Lounging on her bed, Portia complained, "Nerissa, my entire body is tired of this huge world."

Nerissa replied wittily, "Madam, people who have bad luck and no wealth are tired of their life; not those who have everything. You are tired because you have more than you can handle." Portia couldn't help but agree with Nerissa.

"Nerissa, I am a living daughter still controlled by her dead father. I have no say in who I can like and I can't reject who I dislike. I cannot choose a husband for myself. My father is dead, but his commands and wishes aren't."

"Madam, your father was an extremely religious person who got strange ideas near his death.

He knew he was dying. So, in hopes of getting the right husband for you, he prepared a challenge. The suitors who come here to marry you have to choose between a casket of gold, silver and lead. Whoever picks the right one will be your deserving husband."

Portia rolled over and buried her face in a pillow.

Nerissa quietly started cleaning the room. There was an unwelcome silence.

A few minutes later, Nerissa asked Portia to wake up and read out the list of the princely men who had visited Belmont to court her. "You read out the list, and I'll tell you who I genuinely liked," said Portia.

Nerissa sat on the balcony seat and read out the names one by one. "Let's see, so the first one was the Prince of Naples."

"Oh, yes, that prince with his horse. He only talked about horses and their shoes. I think he thought it was a great credit to his character that he could shoe a horse all by himself," Portia rolled her eyes.

Nerissa continued, "Then there was the Count from Palatine. What did you think of him?"

Portia paused for a second which convinced Nerissa that Portia liked him. But, to her surprise, Portia said, "Oh, that guy who always frowned! He looked like he didn't care for my opinion. He didn't smile, much less laugh, at funny stories. He was so solemn the entire time. I can only imagine how much he'll cry in his old age." Nerissa chuckled.

Portia sighed quietly, "I wish I could meet a man with a

golden heart. A person who believes in eternal love."

Nerissa advised Portia not to worry about the princely men as they had already sealed their fates.

"What do you mean?" asked Portia.

Nerissa replied, "They said they wanted to go back home and give up on you until there's another way, a simpler way, of winning over the most beautiful girl in the world."

"I will die an old maid's death unless I can marry someone whom I like. The only thing I like about these suitors is that they are not here; I wish them a happy journey."

Nerissa suddenly remembered a man who had visited Belmont a while ago.

"Madam, do you remember the Venetian scholar and soldier who visited Belmont with Marquess of Montferrat? Your father was still alive then ..."

Portia's face lit up! "Yes, yes! His name was Bassanio, if I remember correctly."

Nerissa nodded, "Yes, madam, I think he is the man who deserves a beauty like you."

Portia blushed. "I remember him. He is a person who deserves such praise."

Just then a servant knocked on the door and informed Portia about the arrival of the Prince of Morocco. She waved him away and asked Nerissa to look after him.

Back in the market, Bassanio and Shylock, a moneylender, were negotiating.

"Three thousand ducats?" asked Shylock.

"Yes, for three months only," replied Bassanio.

"For three months!"

"As I told you, Antonio will guarantee my loan. He will pay the loan if I cannot pay it back on time."

"Antonio is giving the guarantee ... interesting."

"So, what is your answer?"

Shylock iterated the deal, "Three thousand ducats for three months and Antonio is giving the guarantee!"

Bassanio was getting restless. "Your answer ..."

"Antonio is a reliable man," Shylock finally relented.

"Have you heard anything contrary?"

"No, no. That's not what I meant. I meant that he has enough money to repay my loan, but I am worried about his uncertain investments. I heard that one of his ships is bound for Tripoli and another one for the Indies. What's more, people from Rialto tell me that a third ship is in Mexico and the last one in England."

"So?"

"Nothing, it's just that ships are just pieces of wood

and sailors are just men. There are pirates, thieves and storms in the ocean. There's no surety of them returning. However, Antonio is still a reliable merchant. So I can give you a loan based on his guarantee," Shylock declared.

"Shylock, I assure you that Antonio will repay the loan within the given time."

"I will make sure that he does. But before making any commitments, can I meet Antonio?"

Bassanio invited Shylock to dine with them but Shylock refused. "Bassanio you're a Christian and I am a Jew. I can buy from you, walk with you, talk to you and sell to you. But I will never eat, drink or pray with you."

Bassanio frowned, but asked him what he'd prefer instead. Before Shylock could reply, Bassanio spotted Antonio walking towards them.

Shylock's gaze hardened. "I hate him! That timid Christian merchant. He stupidly lends money to people without interest and lowers the interest rate in all of Venice. He has robbed me of my profits and now here he is begging for funds for his dearest friend. The time has come to settle my old grievances against him," he thought.

Bassanio interrupted his reverie, "Shylock, are you even listening to me?"

"Yes, of course, Bassanio," said Shylock. "I just realised that I cannot give you three thousand ducats right away. I don't have that much money right now. But, Tubal, a rich merchant and my dear friend, can help us. For how many months do you want the money again?"

As if just noticing him, Shylock greeted Antonio, "Oh, hello signor! How are you? We were just talking about you."

Antonio replied, "Hello, Shylock. I am well, thank you. Shylock, my reputation of never lending or borrowing money with interest has gotten me this far. But today, for my best friend, I am ready to ruin that reputation!"

Antonio asked Bassanio, "Does he know how much money you need?"

Shylock nodded. "Three thousand ducats."

"For three months," Antonio reminded him.

"Oh, yes, I forgot. He told me," Shylock said absentmindedly.

"Antonio, did you say that you do not lend or borrow money with interest?"

"That's right, I don't."

Shylock clenched his fist in anger. "You know, Antonio, there was once a boy called Jacob. He was responsible for handling his uncle Leban's spotted lambs. Their pay entirely went to him."

> My reputation of never lending or borrowing money with interest has gotten me this far. But today, for my best friend, I am ready to ruin that reputation!

"What's your point, Shylock? Did Jacob charge interest?"

Shylock continued, "No, no. Let me finish the story. When Jacob was given the responsibility, it was the end of autumn—the sheep start mating in this period. So, Jacob planned to increase the number of spotted lambs. He knew that the new-borns look like whatever their mother sees during the time of birth. So, Jacob planted spotted branches in the ground. Later, the lambs gave birth to spotted lambs, which increased his business. It was his way of expanding his business. So what I'm trying to say is that profit is a blessing, unless you steal it."

"Are you trying to say that charging interest is a great business plan?"

"I am just saying that expanding your business is important, and for that interest is vital."

"Shylock, you look like a good apple, but you're rotten at the core," Antonio said bluntly.

Shylock glowered at him. "Signor Antonio, you insult me, you call me a dog, and you spit on my clothes. Yet, I am ready to lend you money. Is that not enough!"

"Shylock, you look like a good apple, but you're rotten at the core."

"Shylock, whenever I meet you again, I'll still refer to you as a dog. So it's better that you lend us the money not as a friend but as an enemy. As an enemy, it will be easier for you to get your money back."

Shylock fired back, "Look at you,

all riled up! I am offering you zero per cent interest, and you're showing me attitude!" He took a deep breath. "I am a kind man. Come with me, let's go to the notary and we'll legally fix this deal. But, I will add a clause, as a joke. If you're unable to return the money at the time we

> If you're unable to return the money at the time we have decided–I'll take a pound of flesh from your body ...

have decided—I'll take a pound of flesh from your body, from whichever part I like."

Antonio was enraged but agreed without a word. However, Bassanio refused to do so. "No, Antonio, you cannot do that! If this is going to be a clause, I'd much rather not have any money."

Antonio reassured Bassanio, "Don't worry, my friend! In two months' time, a month before his deadline, I'll get double the amount of the loan from my investors. I'll pay him well in time."

"Then I'll go home and get the money, you go to the notary and get the clause included in the contract," said Shylock, satisfied.

Bassanio watched him leave suspiciously. "Antonio, I don't like this. He's an evil person pretending to do good."

Back in Belmont, seeing the Prince of Morocco entering her house, Portia tensed. The prince greeted her graciously and said, "Madam, don't hold my dark skin against me. I was simply born and raised in the sun. But I am as red-blooded as any other man."

Portia replied pleasantly, "Good looks aren't all I am looking for, sir. And I assure you, if I weren't tied by my father's conditions, you would have as much of a chance to marry me as any other man."

"Portia, it is my honour to be standing in front of you. I will do anything for you. But if I lose you because of blind luck, or someone worse than me wins, I'll die of sadness," declared the prince.

"Sir, you have to take your chances. Either you don't take the risk at all, or if you lose, promise me that you won't ask for another hand in marriage."

> Oh God, it is my father. He doesn't recognise me because he's partially blind. I'll fool around with him a bit.

Meanwhile, in another part of town, Launcelot was roaming on the streets of Venice, grumbling about his evil master, Shylock.

"Oh, my lord, I want to leave my master Shylock. He is a terrible man. An incarnation of the devil himself! But whenever I think of running away, my heart tells me that I'm wrong. What should I do!"

"Excuse me, sir! Can you please tell me the way to the Jew's residence?" a man asked Launcelot. It was old Gobbo.

Launcelot recognised him instantly. “Oh God, it is my father. He doesn't recognise me because he's partially blind. I'll fool around with him a bit.”

Out loud he said, “Sir, you should turn right at the next turn and then turn left. And then at the next turn, don't turn right or left—go down and around. You'll be at the Jew's house.”

“These directions are confusing. Sir, I am looking for Launcelot, he works there,” said Gobbo.

Launcelot smiled cheekily. “Sir are you talking about Master Launcelot?”

Gobbo shook his head. “No Sir, Launcelot, my son, is from a poor family, and he works there as a servant.”

“Sir, if you are talking about Master Launcelot, then you should know that he is no more,” said Launcelot. Gobbo was shocked! “No, sir, don’t say that. Launcelot was supposed to support me in my old age.”

“What am I, a cane? How can I support you in your old age?” Launcelot snapped.

Gobbo, still unaware that it was Launcelot, pleaded, “Sir, please tell me whether my son is alive or dead.”

“Father, I don't believe this, you still don't recognise me! I am your son. I am the Jew’s servant, and Margery, your wife, is my mother.”

"Oh, my wife's name is Margery! So you really are my son," exclaimed Gobbo.

Gobbo touched Launcelot's face. "You have more hair on your chin than my horse's tail does!"

Gobbo asked Launcelot about his job and his master Shylock. Launcelot confessed, "Father, I am so happy that you met me today. I can't do this anymore. Shylock is a devil. He's starving me to death. I can see my ribs clearly." He added, "Father, Bassanio is coming here. Please talk to him. I want to work for him."

"Good morning, sir," Gobbo greeted Bassanio who accepted the greeting cordially.

"Yes, how can I help you?" asked Bassanio.

"Sir, this is my son, Launcelot. He's a poor boy," said Gobbo.

Launcelot interrupted, "Not a poor boy, sir. Servant of a rich Jewish master, who wants, as my father will explain ..."

Gobbo continued, "He and his master aren't exactly friends ..."

Launcelot interrupted again, "To be precise sir, my master has done me wrong. He wants me to—as my father will tell you."

Gobbo said, "I have this present for you, sir. Please accept it and ..."

Launcelot intervened, "My wish is what this old man will tell you ..."

Bassanio stopped them, "Please, one of you do the talking. I can't understand a thing!"

Launcelot exploded, "I wish to work for you, sir!"

"This is what I was trying to say," said Gobbo.

Bassanio replied, "I know what you want and who you are. I have talked to Shylock. If you want to leave a rich man's service and join a poor master, I am fine with it."

Launcelot thanked Bassanio profusely. "Sir, there is a

proverb that says, 'The grace of gods is enough.' This proverb can be split between you and my master Shylock—you have the grace of gods and Shylock has enough." Bassanio was impressed and asked Launcelot to join him right away.

Bassanio walked ahead to meet Gratiano who requested Bassanio to allow him to accompany him to Belmont. Bassanio agreed on one condition—that Gratiano would behave himself.

At Shylock's home, his daughter Jessica, was saddened by Launcelot leaving, but she wished him luck. She handed him a letter and asked him to deliver it to Lorenzo before leaving. Launcelot accepted the ducats she gave him and left.

At Bassanio's house, Solanio, Gratiano, Lorenzo and Salarino were planning a masquerade ball, when Launcelot entered. Launcelot handed the letter to Lorenzo.

"I am ashamed of being my father's daughter."

Lorenzo opened it and recognised the handwriting immediately. It read,

I am a heinous sinner. I am ashamed of being my father's daughter. But I know that I am only related to his blood, not his behaviour. I'll be a better person than him. Lorenzo, I want to end this agony and become a Christian by marring you soon.

Your dearest,
Jessica

Gratiano observed Lorenzo and said, “I bet it's a love letter!” Launcelot made to leave the room.

Lorenzo stopped Launcelot and asked him to convey a message to Jessica. Launcelot returned to Shylock's house under the pretence of inviting him to the masquerade ball.

As Launcelot announced his resignation, Shylock yelled, “Well, now you'll know how Christians are! You won't get to eat like a pig, or snore, or wear the clothes you did here.”

“Jessica!” Shylock called for his daughter.

“Father, you called me?” Jessica walked in.

“Jessica, Bassanio has invited me to his party tonight. I don't want to go, but I have to.”

He warned her, “Jessica, lock the doors and be careful, those Christians will be on the streets today. Don't open the door for anyone.”

Launcelot whispered to Jessica, “Madam, please be on the lookout. When you are staring out of the window tonight, there might be a Christian coming for you.”

Jessica murmured to herself as Shylock left, "Goodbye, father. Today I'll lose a father, and you, a daughter."

Later that evening, Salarino and Gratiano were waiting for Lorenzo to arrive. "I am amazed that Lorenzo is late. Lovers are usually early!" said Salarino.

Gratiano spotted Lorenzo walking towards them. "Here comes our lover boy!"

"Thank you both for waiting. If someday you have to steal your love from her house, I'll return the favour," said Lorenzo. He asked his friends to stand guard while he talked to Jessica.

"Jessica! It's Lorenzo, your love!" Lorenzo called out.

Jessica appeared at the window. "Lorenzo, catch this box. It'll be worth your while. I am so glad that I could meet you today. I'm glad it's a dark night so you can't see me in my man's disguise."

Lorenzo asked Jessica to come down quickly as she was the torch-bearer for the feast.

Soon, Jessica descended and Gratiano exclaimed, "My God, she is beautiful and too good to be true!"

Lorenzo replied, "I know, I love her! As long as she is herself, she'll always be faithful, wise and beautiful."

Salarino, Gratiano, Lorenzo and Jessica reached Antonio's house and knocked on the door. Antonio opened the door.

"Gratiano, there is to be no party tonight. The wind is blowing right, so Bassanio is leaving for Belmont. I sent twenty people to look for you," he said. Gratiano quickly left for the port to meet Bassanio.

In Belmont, Portia was welcoming the prince to the room of caskets. Portia asked her servants to draw the curtains and presented the caskets to the prince. He stepped closer to the boxes and read the inscriptions on them.

The gold casket said,

He who chooses me,
will win what many men desire.

The silver casket said,

He who chooses me,
will get what he deserves.

The lead casket said,

He who chooses me,
will give and risk all that he has.

The Prince of Morocco was bewildered. "How will I know if I am choosing the right one?"

Portia replied, "One of the caskets contains my photograph. If you choose the correct one, I will be your wife, and if not, then you will remain unmarried."

The prince read all the inscriptions again and deduced, "I do deserve Portia. But men around the world also want her; she is too beautiful to be placed in anything lesser than gold. So, it's decided, I will open the golden casket."

He requested Portia to hand him the keys for the gold box.

The prince opened the box in anticipation and saw a human skull with a scroll placed in its right eye! "What is this, a skull and a scroll!" He was aghast.

> "But men around the world also want her: she is too beautiful to be placed in anything lesser than gold."

Portia requested the prince to read out the message. The scroll read, "Everything that glitters is not gold. I am sure you have heard this saying. If you were as wise and mature as you look, you wouldn't have chosen me. So, goodbye, you have lost your chance."

The prince left, utterly humiliated. Portia asked the

servants to draw the curtains and place everything as it was. She prayed, "I hope whoever looks like him chooses the golden box."

Back in Venice, Salarino and Solanio were having a heated discussion.

"I saw Bassanio and Gratiano sailing on the ship. Lorenzo wasn't there," said Salarino.

"But Shylock got an audience with the duke and took him to the port to search for Lorenzo and Jessica. They ran away last night," Solanio replied.

Salarino filled him in on the events. "Shylock thinks that Bassanio helped them. But the duke confirmed that Lorenzo and Jessica were not on his ship. Apparently they were seen riding a gondola belonging to Antonio."

Solanio mocked Shylock, "I have never seen such a confused man. Today, on the streets, he was screaming that his daughter stole everything from him. Jessica took all the ducats and jewellery from the house. He was crying and people were laughing at his misery."

He sighed. "I hope Antonio repays the loan soon, otherwise he will have to suffer a lot."

"I was talking to a Frenchman yesterday, and he told me that a Venetian ship loaded with treasure was wrecked in the English Channel. I hope it's not Antonio's ship," Salarino said fervently.

Solanio was stunned. "What? Did you tell Antonio about this?"

Salarino hadn't. He didn't wish to be the bearer of bad news.

Solanio entreated him, "Salarino, you have to tell him. But do it gently. The news is upsetting. Antonio is the kindest person I have ever met."

He added, "Today, I saw Antonio saying goodbye to Bassanio. Bassanio promised that he would be back soon, but Antonio asked him to take as much time as he needed, without worrying about the loan; he said he'd handle it."

"I think Antonio loves his life because Bassanio is in it. Come, let's cheer him up," Solanio suggested.

In Belmont, Portia and Nerissa waited for the Prince of Arragon to arrive. Portia welcomed the prince and requested him to open one of the boxes. The prince promised Portia, "I assure you, if I choose the wrong box, I'll never tell anyone about it. Secondly, I will leave the premises right away, and lastly, I will never propose marriage to any other girl."

Portia was impressed and encouraged him to choose. The prince inched closer to the boxes and picked the silver casket. He opened the box and found a picture of an idiot holding a scroll.

It read, "This box was tested by fire seven times. The person who marries my daughter will never fail when tested. But you did. You're as foolish as people with silver hair and silver coins. So stop fooling around and leave immediately."

The prince left, devastated. Portia was also leaving the room when a servant walked in.

"Madam, a messenger has arrived to inform that his lord is on the way. He has brought lots of gifts for you. He seems promising, like spring hinting towards a bright summer."

Portia asked the servant to be quiet and return to the hall. Nerissa mumbled, "I hope it's Bassanio."

In Venice, Salarino and Solanio were once again discussing the news from Rialto.

"What's the news Salarino?"

"The ship that was wrecked today in the English Channel was carrying precious cargo. It sank in the Goodwin sand, a very dangerous sandbar. Many ships have drowned there before," replied Salarino.

Solanio prayed, "I hope Antonio suffers no loss. He is so good and kind."

Salarino said, "We should say 'amen' before a devil comes and interrupts our prayer. Too late, I can see a devil coming here, disguised as a Jew. Hey, Shylock. How are you? Did you hear anything about your daughter?"

Shylock gave him a disgusted look. "No one knows as much as you about my daughter's plan!"

Salarino replied, "Yes, of course. I even know the tailor who made the disguise that she wore when she ran off with Lorenzo!"

Solanio taunted him, "Shylock, I am sure you knew that your daughter was going to run. You generally know when children are ready to leave their parents."

Shylock yelled, "And she will be damned for it! My blood and flesh has revolted against me."

Salarino retorted, "Shylock, your flesh is different from hers. Like ivory and coal. And your blood is as different as red and white wine. Nevertheless, have you heard anything about Antonio's losses at sea?"

“Antonio is another bad deal I have made. He is bankrupt, and he will have to hide his face now,” said Shylock, shaking with anger.

“He used to laugh at my business sense, make fun of my interests, and give loans to Christians as a friend—now he will learn from his mistakes.”

Salarino clenched his fists. “If he cannot pay on time, you won’t cut off his flesh, right? What good would that do to you?”

Shylock narrowed his eyes. “Even if his flesh is of no use to me, it will feed my revenge! Antonio has insulted me time and again, even in public. He riled up my enemies and lowered the interest rates in Venice. He turned my friends against me and humiliated my race. He can’t humiliate

“Antonio is another bad deal I have made. He is bankrupt, and he will have to hide his face now,”

me just because I am a Jew! Are Jews not humans? Does he think we don't have feelings, emotions, five senses and organs? Don't we get sick with the same diseases, get healed by the same medicines? If you prick us, don't we bleed? If you tickle us, don't we laugh? If you poison us, don't we die? And if we insult you, don't you take revenge? So why can't we seek revenge!"

Shylock took a deep breath and said, “Revenge! That is what matters to me. Even if he returns the money, I will not accept it. I want revenge for my suffering.”

Antonio's servant came looking for Salarino. “Sir, Antonio is at home. He is waiting for you.”

Solanio saw Tubal approaching Shylock and sneered, “Another Jew is coming. You cannot find a third devil like them unless Satan himself comes here disguised as a Jew.”

As Solanio and Salarino left for Antonio’s, Shylock enquired about his daughter and Lorenzo, but Tubal had no news about them.

> “Revenge! That is what matters to me. Even if he returns the money, I will not accept it.”

Shylock cried, “She has taken all my wealth—my precious stones, a thousand ducats and my reputation. I wish she were lying dead in front of me wearing those rings. Jessica will be damned! Why am I the only one inflicted with such misery? Nobody suffers but me!”

Tubal tried to comfort him. "Sir, there are more people in Genoa who have really bad luck!"

"Who?"

"Antonio's ship was wrecked while arriving from Tripolis."

Shylock couldn't believe the turn of events; he was overjoyed. "Thank God! Someone is suffering."

"But Shylock, I heard that your daughter spent eighty ducats in one night in Genoa."

Shylock was aghast. "Tubal, now you are sticking a dagger through my heart. Eighty ducats in one go! I'll never see my money now."

To console Shylock, Tubal said, "I talked to other merchants in Venice, and they all agreed that this time it's going to be hard for Antonio to get away. He will go bankrupt eventually."

Shylock perked up once again. But Tubal then said, "A creditor showed me a turquoise ring of yours. Apparently your daughter sold it for a monkey."

"That turquoise ring, my wife gifted it to me. I wouldn't have sold it for a whole jungle of monkeys!" Shylock cried in disdain.

"But Antonio is definitely going to suffer!"

Shylock's eyes lit up. "Tubal, get a police officer ready two weeks before the deadline. If Antonio doesn't pay up, I'll have him arrested and carve his heart out of his chest. And then I can conduct business as I please."

In Belmont, Portia and Nerissa were beaming with happiness. Portia hadn't expected Bassanio to come all the way from Venice to Belmont for her.

Bassanio and Gratiano greeted the ladies. Portia couldn't help but stare at Bassanio. She whispered, "Bassanio, your eyes have bewitched me. It's impossible for me to think of anything else." Nerissa nudged her to come back to reality and greet Bassanio and his friend gracefully.

She said warmly, "Welcome, young men! How are you?" Bassanio smiled and said, "If I have your permission, my lady, can we start the game?"

"Bassanio, why don't you wait for a day or two before you take this risk ..."

"Let me get on with the task, my lady. Waiting is a torture I can't bear right now."

"Oh, torture, is it? Then what are you going to confess?" Portia giggled.

"Only my love," Bassanio grinned.

"Oh, but I'm afraid you're only saying this under pressure. Men will confess to anything under torture!" Her voice softened. "Bassanio, please stay here for a little longer and get to know me before opening those caskets. I want you to win. I don't want to lose you because of sheer bad luck. I wish I could guide you, but that will break my oath. Please don't pick a casket just yet!"

> "Decoration is nothing but a trap for the viewer."

"Pretty lady, I have faith in my love. I promise you that I will not lose. Now, if you will allow me ..." Bassanio smiled reassuringly.

Portia was petrified. She gathered her strength and allowed Bassanio to move forward. Nerissa asked the servants to open the curtains.

As Bassanio walked closer to the caskets, Portia panicked. Her heart was racing with anticipation.

Bassanio stood before the golden box and said, "The way you can't judge a book by its cover or a beautiful lady by her face—I can't judge this golden box by its shine."

Bassanio picked up the golden box and continued, "Decoration is nothing but a trap for the viewer. A beautiful shore can distract a man from the perils of a stormy sea. This box can distract foolish men, but not me."

Bassanio kept the golden box back in its place and moved towards the other caskets. "This silver one is also an illusion. Common coins are made of this metal. But this humble lead box attracts me the most. Although it's too threatening to promise me anything worthy, it has moved me more than I thought it would. I pick the lead one."

He gestured for the key. Portia admired Bassanio as she handed him the key. She fondly mumbled, "All my emotions are vanishing in thin air. Fear, doubt, jealousy and desperation are disappearing. I am falling in love with him. Please, someone, control me, or I am going to overindulge and make myself sick."

Bassanio finally opened the box and in it sat a beautiful picture of Portia! He marvelled at her beauty and said, "Look, I found a photo of this beautiful lady. I wonder if these eyes are moving or if my mind is playing tricks. Her hair, a golden mesh to trap the hearts of men."

Bassanio couldn't stop gazing at her picture. "I can only imagine what the painter went through while painting Portia. He must have been enchanted and unable to paint any other portraits."

Bassanio kept the box aside and read the scroll aloud.

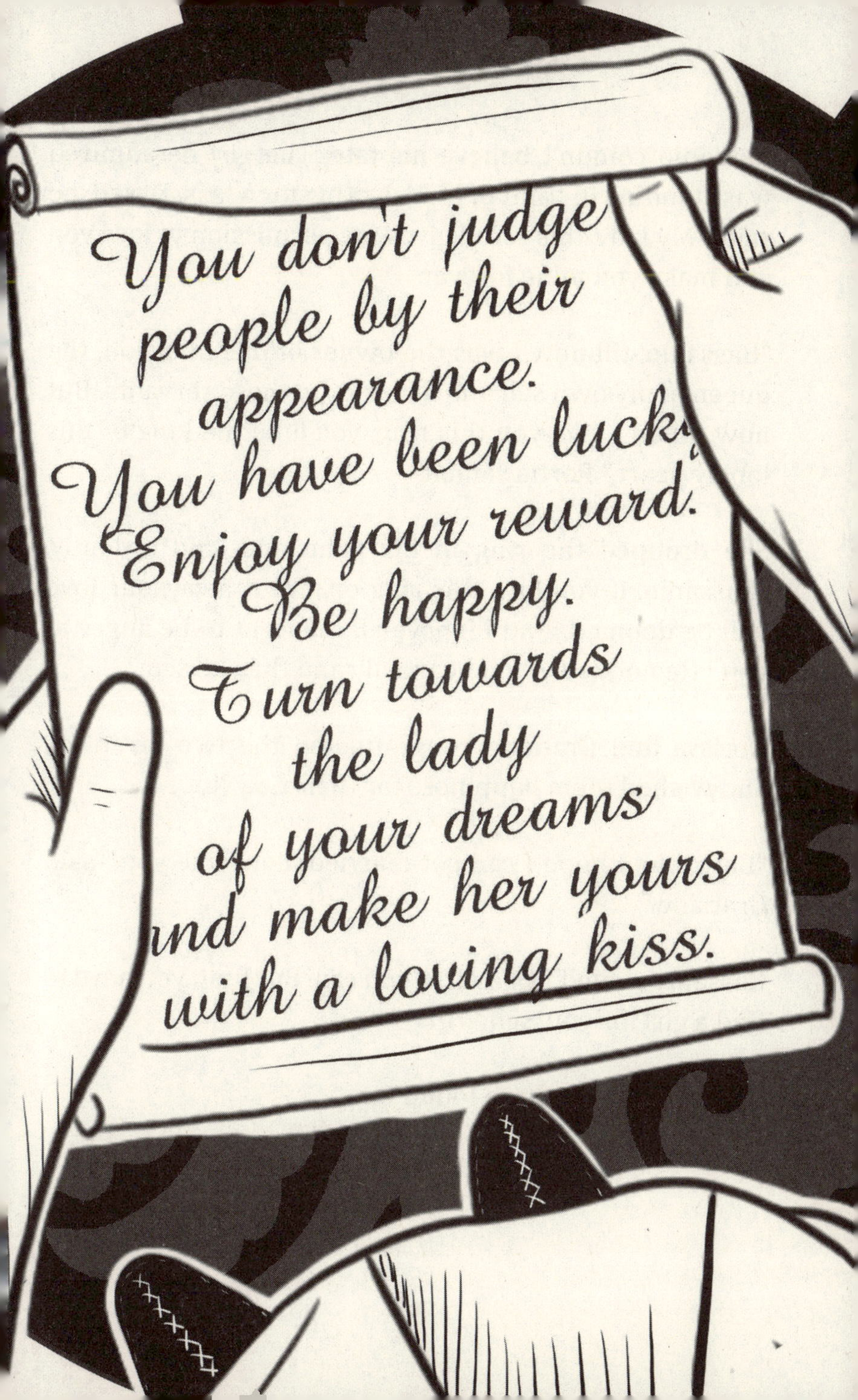
You don't judge
people by their
appearance.
You have been luck
Enjoy your reward.
Be happy.
Turn towards
the lady
of your dreams
nd make her yours
with a loving kiss.

Bassanio couldn't believe his fate. The girl he admired was standing in front of him, waiting for a kiss. Dazed, he said, "My lady, this scroll gives me permission to kiss you and make you mine forever."

"Bassanio, till now I was the owner of this mansion, the queen of my own self and a master to these servants. But now, when I give you this ring, you'll be the king of this lonely heart," Portia sighed.

She dropped the ring in his palm and said ardently, "Bassanio, if you lose this ring or give it away, our love will be doomed. And I'll have all the right to be angry at you." He nodded wholeheartedly and they kissed.

Nerissa and Gratiano congratulated the two lovebirds and wished them happiness for their new life.

"Bassanio, I hope I can get married alongside you," said Gratiano.

Bassanio smiled. "Of course you can. But first, you have to find a girl for yourself."

"I think I already have found one."

> “Bassanio, if you lose this ring or give it away, our love will be doomed.”

Bassanio was bewildered. “Gratiano, what are you trying to say?”

Gratiano started hesitantly, “I love Nerissa ... and I believe she loves me too. She took her time to reciprocate my love for her but, finally, she has agreed. However, she'll only marry me if you and Portia get married.” Portia and Bassanio gladly accepted their love.

Meanwhile, Lorenzo, Salarino and Jessica entered the room. “Welcome, my friends,” said Bassanio, looking at Portia out of the corner of his eye.

Portia grinned, “Bassanio, this is your house now. You can do as you wish!”

Lorenzo congratulated Bassanio and Portia. “Bassanio, I had no intention of visiting, but Salerio saw us and invited us to come here. I hope you don't mind.”

"No, Lorenzo, not at all," Bassanio replied warmly.

Salerio stepped forward and handed over a letter to Bassanio. "Signor, this is from Antonio."

At once colour drained from Bassanio's face. "Is Antonio okay?"

"Sir, you should read it for yourself. His health is fine, but he is distraught."

Bassanio unfolded the letter and a tear rolled down his cheek. The moment the first tear fell from his eyes, the rest followed like an unbroken stream.

Portia couldn't bear the sight of her future husband in such pain. "Bassanio, what's wrong? What has made you so pale and sad?"

> Now Antonio's businesses have failed and he is left with nothing.

"Portia, when I told you that I am a wealthy man and money runs in my veins—it was true. But when I said that I am not worthy of your love, I was not being humble. When I came here, I didn't have enough money of my

own. So, my best friend loaned me some money, but for that he took a loan from his mortal enemy, Shylock. Now Antonio's businesses have failed and he is left with nothing." Bassanio choked up again.

He finally gathered himself and said, "But Salerio, his ships went to many different places—Tripolis, Indies, England, Lisbon, North America and Mexico. Not even a single ship could survive?"

Salerio nodded gravely. "Sir, even if Signor Antonio had the amount ready, Shylock wouldn't accept it. He wants his revenge. He wants a pound of Antonio's flesh. In fact, twenty noblemen, countrymen, merchants and the duke himself have tried to persuade him to forgo the contract, but Shylock is adamant on fulfilling his wish."

Jessica chimed in, "When I was in that house with Shylock, I heard him conspiring with Tubal and Cush, his countrymen. He will not leave Antonio even for thirty thousand ducats! I don't think Antonio has any chance till the law intervenes."

"How much does Antonio owe Shylock?" Portia asked Bassanio.

"Three thousand ducats."

Portia replied simply, "So you pay him six thousand ducats and get your friend back. Take the money from mc. But before that, can I please read the letter?"

Bassanio handed the letter to Portia. It said,

Dear Bassanio,
Unfortunately all my businesses have collapsed, but I have cleared all your dues, as promised. However, if your affection for me doesn't convince you, you can consider this letter a mere piece of paper.

Portia urged Bassanio to leave as soon as possible after holding a small wedding ceremony in the church. "I can live without you for a few days but I cannot see you losing sleep while lying right beside me. So let's hurry up and get married, dear Bassanio."

In Venice, Antonio's efforts to change Shylock's decision were all going in vain. Nevertheless, he was not ready to give up.

Solanio cursed Shylock, "He is the most stubborn dog who has ever lived amongst humans!"

Antonio sighed, "Solanio, it's fine. I will not run after him with my pleas any more. I know why he's doing this; he hates me because I lend money to the poor without charging any interest."

"Antonio, you don't deserve this. But you must not worry. The duke will not listen to his plea or consider his contract valid."

"Solanio, the duke won't deny the law. If he did, it would threaten the security of the foreign merchants in Venice, and that is how the city earns money. Don't expect anything from the duke." Antonio suddenly felt unwell.

"I have already lost most of my weight because of the creditors. I have no flesh left for Shylock to peel off my body. But I want Bassanio here to see me pay off his loan. I want to meet him one last time. Then my mind will be at rest," said Antonio, defeated.

Meanwhile, Portia and Nerissa were brainstorming ways to save Antonio from Shylock.

Lorenzo approached Portia and said, "Madam, I hope you don't mind me saying that I respect what you did for Antonio and Bassanio. It was a beautiful gesture of love."

Portia never blushed, but Lorenzo's compliment tainted her cheeks pink. She took a moment to compose herself. "I have heard that one's friends define them. Antonio has risked his life for my husband. I will not let anything happen to him. Lorenzo, I need a favour from you. Could you please take over the management of this house till my husband returns?"

"I have heard that one's friends define them. Antonio has risked his life for my husband. I will not let anything happen to him."

Lorenzo was confused. "But, Madam—"

"Lorenzo, I have sworn that till my husband is back I'll live a life of prayer and contemplation. I'll stay in the monastery nearby, and Nerissa will accompany me. It's the only way I won't spend all my time worrying. I hope you understand."

"Madam, I hope you find peace and happiness. I'll handle everything over here." Portia thanked Lorenzo profusely and left the mansion immediately. She met her messenger Balthasar and asked him to deliver a letter to her cousin Bellario, a Doctor of Law in Padua.

Portia asked Nerissa to pack her bags; they were going to meet Bassanio in Venice. Nerissa was bewildered by Portia's instructions. "Madam, what are you planning to do?"

"Nothing much. We'll meet them in Venice disguised as men. They won't even recognise us," said Portia, giggling.

Meanwhile, the duke was announcing poor Antonio's penalty in the courtroom in Venice. However, he was reluctant to declare the order. "Antonio, I am very sorry that you have to face this ruthless enemy. I tried everything, but he refuses to budge."

Antonio replied compassionately, "Sir, I know that you have tried your best. I appreciate your efforts. I am now ready to face anything. Bring him in."

The duke requested one of his servants to call Shylock into the courtroom.

Shylock entered and the duke asked everyone to make room for him, and made him stand in front of Antonio.

The duke said, "Shylock, everyone here hopes that you will show some mercy for this poor man. They believe that you will, in the end, absolve Antonio from your penalty; that you're just pretending to be cruel."

His brows wrinkled into a scowl. "I also hope that you will waive some portion of the principal he owes you, considering his recent losses."

Shylock replied firmly, "Sir, I have told you what I intend to do. I want my penalty, which is long due now. And if you refuse me, your city's freedom and charter will be in danger. If you want the reason for my rigidity, then I have already told you, but I'll remind you again – it is my wish. I want to see Antonio in pain. Sir, there is no sense in explaining the reason behind people's likes and dislikes. Some people don't like roasted pig, while others love eating it. Some people can't stand cats, whereas others think they're quite harmless.

Therefore, my reason behind punishing Antonio is my self-satisfaction. I don't want to give any other reason for my penalty. I hope that's okay with you. Now, will you proceed with the case?"

Bassanio screamed, "Your answer doesn't excuse your ruthless behaviour, you cruel man!"

"I don't have to answer your questions or give you answers that you like," Shylock waved him away.

"Not everyone wants to kill those whom they don't like," Bassanio fired back.

"No, but is there anyone who doesn't want to kill whom they hate?"

"Not liking someone and hating them is different, Shylock."

"What! Would you let a snake bite you twice?" Shylock winked at Bassanio roguishly.

Having had enough of Bassanio and Shylock's argument, the now frail Antonio requested the duke to give the ruling as soon as possible.

Bassanio choked up looking at Antonio's condition and requested Shylock to accept six thousand ducats instead of three thousand in exchange for mercy.

"Even if you offer three times the price, I will not accept it. I want what I asked for!" Shylock demanded.

The duke thundered, "Shylock, you're so ruthless! How can you ever hope for mercy when you don't have any to give?"

Shylock was now losing his cool. "Sir, why should I be afraid of your judgement? Antonio is the one who couldn't repay the loan on time. Many of you behave worse than animals with your slaves—why? You believe you own them. You don't let them have the same food as yours; you don't give them the same mattress as yours. Why? It's because you know you own them! So the pound of flesh that I want is my possession. I have paid a heavy price for it. Therefore, I want it."

"It's because you know you own them! So the pound of flesh that I want is my possession."

The duke was waiting for Bellario, the Doctor of Law, to arrive from Padua and help Antonio walk free.

A servant announced, "Sir, a messenger is waiting outside with a letter from Padua."

The duke ordered for him to be let in. Meanwhile, Bassanio was talking to Antonio softly, trying to console him. But Antonio had lost all hope and was begging Bassanio to let him die.

"Antonio, I'll give the Jew my flesh, bones and blood before he touches you. Trust me!" cried Bassanio.

Nerissa entered the courtroom disguised as a lawyer's clerk. The duke asked her, "Are you from Bellario's office?"

"Yes, sir."

Shylock suddenly started sharpening his knife on the sole of his shoe. Bassanio accosted Shylock, "Why are you sharpening your knife? You arrogant jerk!"

Shylock stood up straight, took a deep breath and exhaled slowly. "To cut my deserved penalty from your friend's body."

The duke called the court to order and informed everyone that Bellario had sent one of his colleagues to handle the case. According to him, his colleague was well-versed in law and was familiar with the case.

Portia entered the room, disguised as Balthasar, a male lawyer sent by Bellario. The duke welcomed her.

Portia looked around the room and asked, "Where is the merchant and where is the Jew?" The duke requested Antonio and Shylock to come forward.

Without wasting any more time, Portia commenced the proceeding. "Shylock, your case is unusual. But the Venetian law cannot deny you justice. Antonio, he has a claim on you, correct?"

Antonio nodded.

Portia further asked, "Do you acknowledge the contract?"

Antonio replied, "Yes, I do."

"Great, then Shylock must show you mercy!"

Shylock snapped, "Why should I show him mercy?"

Portia narrowed her eyes. "Well, Shylock, you are not obliged to show mercy to someone. You just do it. It's called humanity. Reconsider your decision, Jew!"

"I take full responsibility for my decision. I want justice; I want the penalty to be fulfilled. Duke, you promised me!"

"Show me the contract you made with Antonio." Shylock handed over the papers to Portia.

Portia read the contract thoroughly. "Shylock, they are offering you thrice the amount you loaned them. What is the problem?"

Shylock shook his head defiantly and requested Portia to deliver justice.

Antonio shrieked, "I beg the court to deliver justice soon!"

Portia nodded gravely. "Antonio, bare your chest!"

A sinful smile appeared on Shylock's face as he picked up his knife and scale for measurement.

Portia requested the servant to get a surgeon to stand by Antonio. Shylock was seething. "What? That's not mentioned anywhere in the contract!"

"Yes, not explicitly, but can't you be a little charitable!"

Portia turned to Antonio. "Are you ready?"

Antonio grabbed Bassanio's hand and bid him farewell.

"Antonio, I married the girl I love because of you. I can sacrifice myself and her for your life. But I will not let you go," Bassanio wept.

Portia glared at Bassanio. "You are sacrificing your wife behind her back. It might make her unhappy."

She beckoned Shylock to come forward. "Before we begin, this contract states that you can cut his flesh, but if you spill even a drop of his blood, the court of Venice will confiscate your property and land."

Shylock was gobsmacked. "What are you saying? That's not written anywhere!"

Portia handed him the papers and asked him to check them.

Shylock knew he had been beaten. "Fine, give me thrice the amount, and I'll let Antonio go!" Bassanio was about to hand him the money, but Portia stopped him. “No, you refused the money. You’re getting your penalty. What's wrong, Shylock?”

“Just give me the money and let me go.”

“You cannot take the nine thousand ducats anymore. We gave you a chance, but it’s too late now.”

“Well then, I hope he chokes on them! I am not staying here to argue with you.” Shylock made to storm out.

“Wait,” said Portia. “You can't leave like this. According to the laws of Venice, if a foreigner tries to kill a citizen, directly or directly, he will have to pay a penalty. Jew, you have to give half your property to Antonio and the other half to the State. The duke will decide if you live.”

Antonio intervened, “I request the State to pardon one half of his property. And the other I will accept only to bequeath it onto his daughter and son-in-law. First, Shylock must promise to immediately become a Christian, and second, his property should be transferred to Lorenzo and Jessica when he dies.”

“Shylock, do you agree?” Portia asked. He nodded, resigned.

Bassanio and Antonio rushed towards Portia with gratitude, still unaware of her real identity.

"I want to give you the three thousand ducats for your brilliant effort. I insist!" said Bassanio.

"I will always be indebted to you. No amount of money can match up to what you have done for us. You can have anything, just ask," Antonio insisted.

"Fine, if you insist, I'll take that ring on your finger." Portia pointed towards Bassanio's ring.

Bassanio apologised and explained the value of the ring, but Portia wasn't ready to negotiate. Offended, she stormed out.

Antonio implored Bassanio to give the ring to Balthasar. He sighed and handed over his ring to Gratiano.

Gratiano ran after the gentlemen and gifted Portia Bassanio's ring and Nerissa his own ring.

Antonio decided to accompany Bassanio to Belmont, eager to meet the lovely Portia. That afternoon, Portia and Nerissa left for Belmont in order to reach home before Bassanio.

In Belmont, Jessica and Lorenzo were enjoying their new life together in Portia's mansion when they received news of Portia and Nerissa arriving home. Jessica asked the servant to prepare a grand feast for all of them.

Soon, Nerissa and Portia arrived. Jessica welcomed them heartily, “Hello, madam. I hope you were able to live peacefully in the monastery.” Portia nodded serenely.

She turned to Nerissa. “Instruct the servants not to mention our trip to Bassanio.”

That evening, trumpeters and musicians gathered for the grand entry of Bassanio and Antonio. Portia walked out to greet Antonio and said, “Sir, I hope your trip to Belmont was comfortable.” He smiled warmly at Portia's gracious welcome.

On the other end, Gratiano and Nerissa were having a heated discussion. "Nerissa, I swear on you—I gave my ring to the lawyer's clerk. He asked for it, I couldn't say no!"

Portia interrupted them, "What are you two fighting about?

Gratiano explained, "Madam, she gave me a ring inscribed with a poem that said 'Love me and never leave me'."

Nerissa rolled her eyes. "It was my love for you, not just a round band."

Gratiano continued, "I gave it to the clerk who came with the lawyer as a reward for saving Antonio."

"Gratiano, the ring was given to you by your love, you shouldn't have given it away so thoughtlessly." Portia glared at Bassanio and continued, "I also gave a ring to Bassanio, and I'm sure he is wearing my gift ever so lovingly."

Bassanio murmured to himself, "Maybe I should cut off my left hand and tell her that I lost the ring while trying to save my hand."

Gratiano promptly said, "Bassanio also gave his ring to the lawyer. He should be punished too!" Portia turned to her husband. "Bassanio, which ring did you give?"

Bassanio avoided her gaze. Portia acted furious and demanded he stay away from her until he gets the ring back.

All of them fell into an intense argument.

Antonio tried to put an end to it. “Ladies, I am sorry, this mess is because of me. But I guarantee Bassanio will never break an oath again.”

Portia took Antonio’s hand and told him he was now Bassanio’s guarantor. She placed a ring in his hand. Bassanio was stunned—it was his ring! Portia finally confessed and smugly recounted their adventure. Antonio thanked Portia profusely. Nerissa informed Lorenzo and Jessica that their fortunes had turned. The couple was pleasantly surprised.

Lorenzo said, “Madam, you have dropped bread from heaven for starving people.”

After a while, Jessica and Lorenzo left for their home in Venice. Nerissa and Gratiano continued living happily in the mansion.

However, the happiest couple was Portia and Bassanio.

After all, they had gotten what they desired and deserved!

The quality of mercy is not strained.
It droppeth as the gentle rain from heaven
Upon the place beneath. It is twice blessed:
It blesseth him that gives and him that takes.
'Tis mightiest in the mightiest. It becomes
The thronēd monarch better than his crown.
His scepter shows the force of temporal power.

– **Portia**, Act IV, Scene 1

The Merchant of Venice

The Merchant of Venice, written by William Shakespeare, is an excellent example of Shakespeare's tragic comedies, where the central conflict of the drama finds resolution before real harm befalls anyone. This tragic comedy, also known as 'problem comedy', is set in the sixteenth century, portraying themes like Man vs. Man, Man vs. Society, and Man vs. Himself.

The play revolves around a central theme of conflict between self-interest, selflessness, friendship and love. This theme drives the plot and the actions of the main characters. Other identifiable themes are greed, hatred, revenge, mercy, appearance vs. reality, worth, lack of control and prejudice. Deception and disguise are two of the central plots of the play. The spiteful behaviour of the Jews and Christians with each other also depicts the feud that is universal and has remained relevant to every society through the years.

Themes

Humanity vs Inhumanity

One of the major themes in *The Merchant of Venice* is Humanity vs. Inhumanity, of which various characters accuse each other. For instance, while insulting and abusing Shylock for his business tactics, the Venetians frequently belittle him as an animal and a devil. In return, Shylock seeks to reduce his debtor, Antonio, to the status of a slave whose soul and body can be bought and butchered. In fact, in the courtroom scene, Shylock likens carving a pound of Antonio's flesh to Venetians owning livestock and slaves.

Prejudice vs Intolerance

The Merchant of Venice particularly talks about the prejudice and extreme intolerance against Jews in Venice. It is possible to argue that Shylock was forced to be shrewd and cunning due to the society's prejudices against him. Shakespeare is subtly criticizing the prejudices of all his characters. For example, Shylock is criticized for charging interest, however it was the discrimination (and possibly the foreign trade laws) that led Shylock to do so. Shylock therefore insists on believing that he learnt his hatred from the society itself.

Revenge, Mercy and Law

Shylock's desire to take revenge on Antonio and the love story of Bassanio and Portia are the central plots that explore themes like law, revenge and mercy.

Though law and revenge are technically conflicting concepts, they tend to overlap. In the story, Shylock tries to exact his revenge by sticking to the law. It is an act of horror within the justice system. When the chance comes for him to show mercy, he refuses it. In contrast, Portia, Antonio and Bassanio show mercy on Shylock by only confiscating his land and wealth, when they could have sentenced him to a harsher punishment. The act of leaving Shylock alive may seem like mercy, yet he carries the burden of this "kindness" for the rest of his days.

Answer me!

Q1. Discuss the character of Antonio.

Q2. Explain the character development of Bassanio in the story. Give examples.

Q3. Was there any character development in Shylock? Give examples.

Q4. Do you think Shylock contemplates Antonio's death when he proposes the clause about a pound of his flesh? If yes, give reasons.

Q5. Compare the characters of Portia and Jessica.

Q6. According to you, which scene in the story is highly dramatized?

Q7. Does the name *The Merchant of Venice* justify the storyline? If you were to give an alternative title to the story, what would it be?

Q8. Describe the friendship between Antonio and Bassanio. Do you think Antonio would have actually given his life for Bassanio during the trial?

Q9. In not more than 500 words, rewrite the story of *The Merchant of Venice.*

Q10. How was Bassanio's logic different from the princes of Morocco and Arragon while choosing a casket?

Q11. Rewrite the beginning of the story in your own words with only two characters, Antonio and Shylock.

Q12. Describe the importance of Nerissa's character in the story. Support your answer with examples.

Q13. Describe the conflict between mercy and justice in the trial scene.

Q14. Discuss a few societal norms and conventions that run the city of Venice in *The Merchant of Venice*.

Q15. "Bassanio you know I would lend you the money if I could. But all of my fortune is tied up in the cargo business, and all the ships are at sea. I'll get my profit when the ships reach the ports. Till then, I can only help you with my words." Who is talking here and why is he asking for time?

Q16. Explain the importance of the following characters in the story: Gratiano, Lorenzo and Launcelot.

Q17. Explain the ending of the story in not more than 200 words.

Q18. Read the abstract below and answer the following questions:

"This box was tested by fire seven times. The person who marries my daughter will never fail when tested. But you did. You're as foolish as people with silver hair and silver coins. So stop fooling around and leave immediately."

- Who is the speaker?
- Who is the listener?
- What was the end result of this?

Q19. Write what you would have done if you were in Shylock's position. Would you have taken revenge on Antonio or would you have remained ethical in your business practices?

The end.